The Three
Little Pigs

Once upon a time, there were three little pigs. They were brave. They were bold. But they weren't very big.

One fine day the little pigs set off to see the world.

Goodbye, Mother!

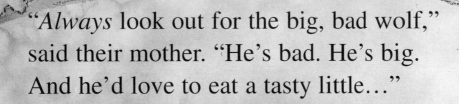

"*Always* look out for the big, bad wolf,"
said their mother. "He's bad. He's big.
And he'd love to eat a tasty little…"

The three little pigs hadn't gone far when they met a man carrying a heavy load of straw.

"I could build a very fine house with that straw," said the first little pig.

And he did.

The two little pigs set off, leaving their brother at his house of straw.

Before long a man came by, with sticks on his back piled ever so high.

"I could build a very fine house with those sticks," said the second little pig.

And she did.

The last little pig set off, leaving his sister at her house of sticks. Soon he met a man carrying a load of bricks.

"I could build a very fine house with those bricks," said the third little pig.

And he did.

Meanwhile, who was creeping up to the house of straw? It was...

It's hard work!

…the big, bad wolf!

"Little pig, little pig, let me come in!"
he growled.

"No! By the hairs on my chinny chin chin,
I won't let you in!" squeaked the first
little pig.

"Then I'll HUFF and I'll PUFF

and I'll blow your house down!" roared the wolf.

Help!

And he did. That was the end of the first little pig.

Next the wolf crept up to the house of sticks.

"Little pig, little pig, let me come in!"
he growled.

"No! By the hairs on my chinny chin chin,
I won't let you in!" squeaked the second
little pig.

"Then I'll HUFF and I'll PUFF and I'll blow your house down!", roared the wolf.

Help!

And he did. That was the end of the second little pig.

Next the wolf crept up to the house of bricks.

"Little pig, little pig, let me come in!" he growled.

"No! By the hairs on my chinny chin chin, I won't let you in!" squeaked the third little pig.

I'm safe in here!

So the wolf *HUFFED* and he *PUFFED*…

and he *HUFFED* and he *PUFFED*…

but he couldn't blow down the house of bricks.

"Little pig," called the wolf, "be ready at six o'clock tomorrow morning, and we'll gather some tasty turnips."

The little pig knew that the wolf planned to eat him. So off he set at *five* o'clock. He filled his basket with tasty turnips and hurried home for six o'clock.

"Bother!" growled the wolf.

"Little pig," called the wolf, "be ready at five o'clock tomorrow morning, and we'll pick some juicy apples."

So the little pig set off at *four* o'clock. He filled his basket with juicy apples and hurried home for five o'clock.

"BOTHER!" roared the wolf.

"Little pig," called the wolf, "be ready at four o'clock this afternoon, and we'll go to the fair."

As soon as the wolf went away, the little pig set off for the fair. He had SO much fun!

ROLL UP!
ROLL U

At four o'clock the wolf arrived.

Just then, the little pig rolled back from the fair inside a barrel. And he bowled right over the wolf!

Quickly the little pig ran indoors.

Now the wolf was *really* angry. He climbed onto the roof.

"Little pig, I'm coming to EAT YOU UP!" he shouted down the chimney.

Indoors, the pig put a pot of water on to boil…

Suddenly the wolf fell down the chimney into the pot of boiling water with a…

CRASH! and a SPLASH!

And that was the end of the big, bad wolf.

And the little pig said, "Now I can live happily ever after in my very fine house of bricks!"

And he did!

Home, sweet home!